THE LEGEND B

Adapted by Trey King

SCHOLASTIC INC.

ISBN 978-0-545-51750-8

LEGO, the LEGO logo, the Brick and Knob configurations, the Minifigure and LEGENDS OF CHIMA are trademarks of the LEGO Group. ©2013 The LEGO Group. Produced by Scholastic Inc. under license from the LEGO Group.
Published by Scholastic Inc. SCHOLASTIC and associated logos are trademarks and/or registered trademarks of Scholastic Inc.

12 11 10 9 8 7 6 5 4 3 2   13 14 15 16 17 18/0

Printed in the U.S.A.   40
First printing, May 2013

The friends sneak inside.

Whoa. Will you look at that?

Yeah, great. Let's go before a guard spots us.

Hey! Put that back! The rules say we're too young for CHI. This is *really* bad!

Cragger uses the CHI!

Cragger! *No!*

Suddenly, Cragger is hit by a stun beam!

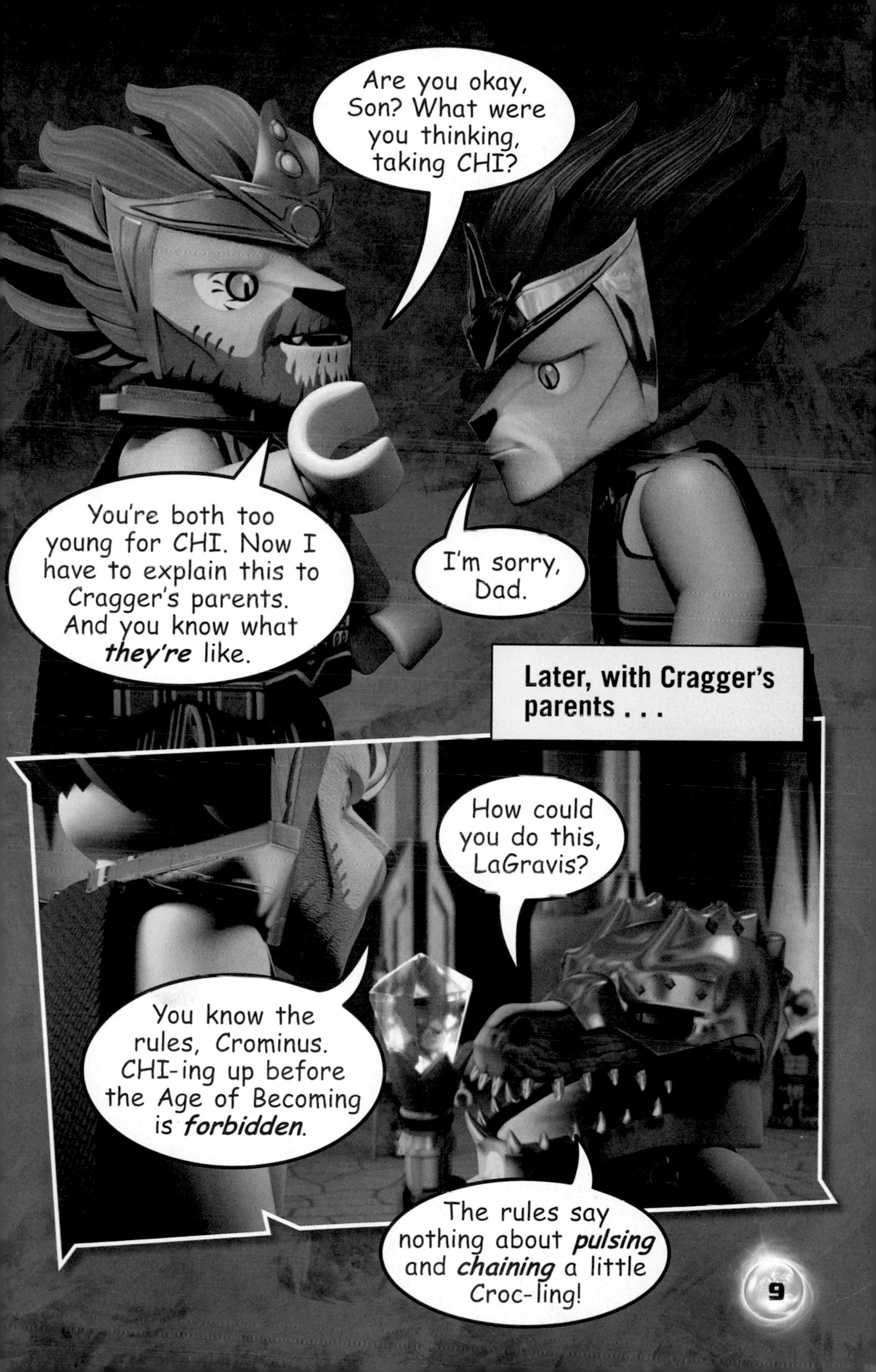

Are you okay, Son? What were you thinking, taking CHI?
You're both too young for CHI. Now I have to explain this to Cragger's parents. And you know what *they're* like.
I'm sorry, Dad.
Later, with Cragger's parents . . .
How could you do this, LaGravis?
You know the rules, Crominus. CHI-ing up before the Age of Becoming is ***forbidden***.
The rules say nothing about ***pulsing*** and ***chaining*** a little Croc-ling!

For a thousand years, the Lions have watched over the Pool of CHI. We ensure it is used properly by ***all*** in Chima. What your son did was not proper.
This isn't over, LaGravis. We Crocodiles ***never*** forget.

A few weeks later, back at the Sacred Pool . . .

I need that CHI. I didn't mean to get Laval in trouble. But I can't stop thinking about the power. . . .

Huh? It's not what you think. I was just, uh, it was all *Laval's* idea.

Really? Because I haven't been allowed out of my room in weeks.

Hey! Get back here!

Fire the *Clawpoon*!

The Clawpoon hits a Lion Vehicle!

Dad! We've got to stop this!

Get down, Laval!

Suddenly, the Croc Vehicle flips over!

15

It starts to fall into a sinkhole!

Cragger calls to the Lions.

Stop fighting! The ground is *unstable*! Please, blame me, not them. *My parents are stuck inside!*

LaGravis tries to pull up the Croc Vehicle . . .

BONK

TUMBLE

Don't worry, my queen. We'll get out of here eventually.

But what about Cragger?

He knows the Lions are not to blame. He'll do the right thing—as long as he doesn't listen to his *sister*.

Be patient with him, Son. He lost both his parents. And he's now king, with a whole tribe to run.

As Lions, we must maintain the *peace* and *balance* of Chima. It is our Sacred Duty, given to us by Nature itself.

Uh-oh. I feel *the Great Story* coming on again.

Once, many centuries ago, there were no buildings or vehicles or tribes in Chima. Just jungles and plains and simple creatures.

One day, the sky opened up and blessed the land, pulling Mount Cavora from the heart of Chima.

The water that flowed from this mountain was different. Full of a life-force we now call *CHI*.

Those who drank from it evolved.

However, some in Chima chose **not** to embrace the CHI. They stayed simple and pure, vanishing into the Outlands.

These creatures are now known as **The Legend Beasts**. It is said they will return one day, when Chima needs them most.

Today, the CHI is collected at the Lion Temple, where it forms into powerful orbs. We Lions are its Sacred Guardians, ensuring that it is shared fairly by **all**.

Once a month, we distribute the orbs to every tribe. But there's always one extra-powerful Golden CHI Orb.
Which we compete for!

Welcome, citizens of Chima! The Golden CHI has chosen this month's contest to be: a ***Joust of Jungle Judgment***! Safeties and blunters on!

Laval chases Cragger to the Falling Jungle and the two battle!

Now it's just you and me, Laval. I'm going to *bury* you, like you did to my parents!

Hey, come on. I'm sorry you lost your parents. But that was all an *accident*!

Cragger slices the tree branch Laval is on!

Craggerrrr. . . !

WHIP!

Hey! Who snaked my spear?

A little birdy did, with some big, metal eggs!

Dude, you got some tree on your shirt. Let me help you there.

That night, at the Croc Swamp, Cragger hatches a plan for revenge.
Worriz. So good to see you.
Enough with the small talk, Cragger. Just tell me how I can *destroy* Laval and the Lions. No one mocks a Wolf in a Speedor race like they did.
Okay, down to business. We attack the Lions during their next Age of Becoming ceremony.
After everything they've done—mark my words—we will make them pay.
To be continued . . .